You may *think* you know this story I am going to tell you, but you have not heard it for true. I was there. So I will tell you the truth of it. Here. Now.

W9-BYK-664

DIAMOND HILLJARVIS BRANCH LIBRARY
CHILDREN 398.2 SAN SOUCI
San Souci, Robert D.
Cendrillon : a Caribbean
Cinderella /
JUN 1 7 2002

For Mom, once again (as always) with love
—R. S. S.

To Andrea and Chloe
—B. P.

Cendrillon
A Caribbean Cinderella

Robert D. San Souci   ILLUSTRATED BY Brian Pinkney

FORT WORTH PUBLIC LIBRARY

Aladdin Paperbacks   New York   London   Toronto   Sydney   Singapore

J live on a green–green island in the so-blue *Mer des Antilles,* the Caribbean Sea. Long ago, when I was a child, my family was poor. When my mother died, she left me only one thing: a wand of mahogany. "Three taps will change one thing into another," my mother had whispered. "But only for a short time. And the magic must be used to help someone you love."

Of what use was this to an orphan like me, who every day struggled to find shelter and fill her belly? I could not use the wand. I had no one to love and no one who loved me.

When I grew up, I worked as a *blanchisseuse,* a washerwoman, scrubbing other people's sheets and shirts at the riverside. Drying them in the sun.

One woman I worked for was kind. I often nursed her, for she was always sickly, poor creature. In thanks, she made me the *nannin'*, godmother, of her baby girl, Cendrillon. When I held that *bébé* in my arms on her christening day, I felt such love! And I saw love returned from her sweet brown eyes.

Alas! Cendrillon's mamma died soon after this. Then her papa, Monsieur, married again. Madame Prospèrine was a cold woman, and puffed-up proud because her grandfather had come from France.

When a new daughter, Vitaline, was born, Madame gave a christening party for her rich friends. What a feast it was!

Madame and the other fine ladies were dressed in satin and velvet, all the colors of the rainbow. They laughed at my worn white skirts and peasant's way of speaking.

Pretty Cendrillon came and kissed me. *"Bonjou', Nannin'."* She gave me a cup of punch. Her hands were blistered and red.

"*Pauv' ti Cendrillon,* poor little child!" I cried. "What have you done to yourself?"

She shrugged. "My father's wife works me like a serving-girl."

"And Monsieur allows this?"

Sighing, she said, "He fears Madame. But I am strong. The work hurts my hands but not my heart."

"Someday, I will find a way to help." Even as I spoke them, my words sounded hollow. What could I—a poor washerwoman—do for my dearest?

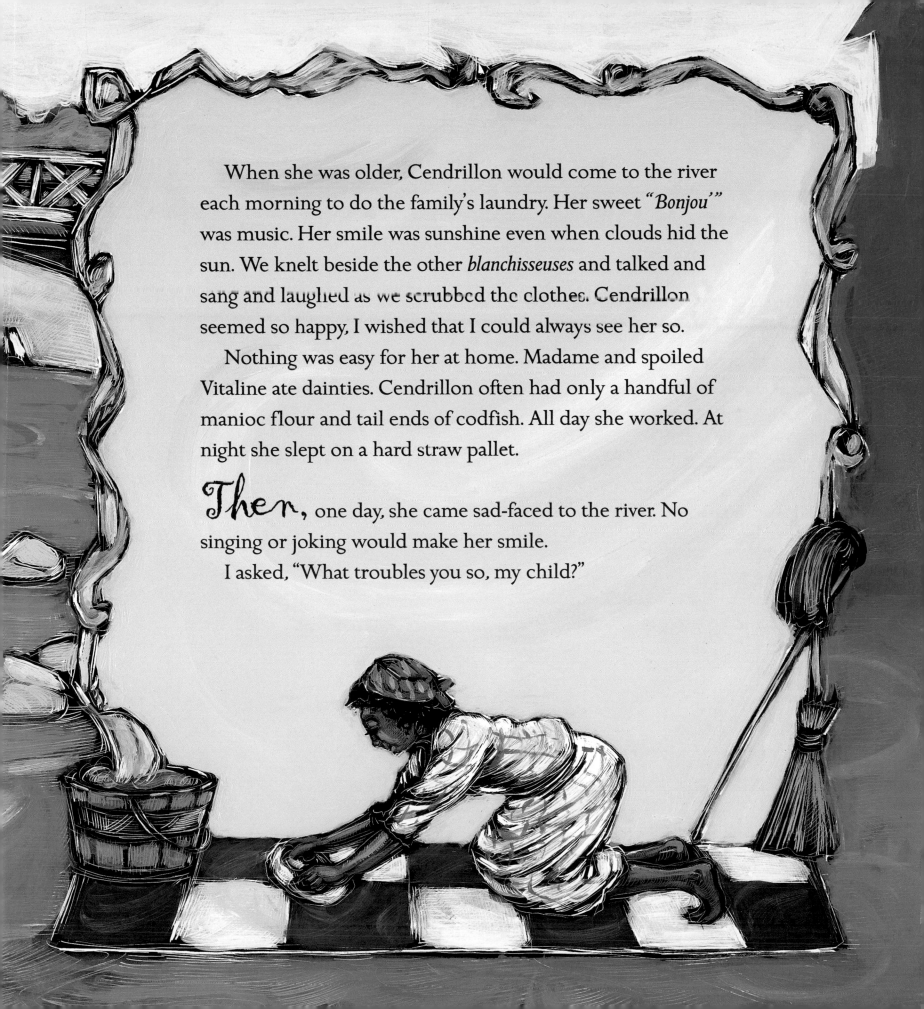

When she was older, Cendrillon would come to the river each morning to do the family's laundry. Her sweet *"Bonjou'"* was music. Her smile was sunshine even when clouds hid the sun. We knelt beside the other *blanchisseuses* and talked and sang and laughed as we scrubbed the clothes. Cendrillon seemed so happy, I wished that I could always see her so.

Nothing was easy for her at home. Madame and spoiled Vitaline ate dainties. Cendrillon often had only a handful of manioc flour and tail ends of codfish. All day she worked. At night she slept on a hard straw pallet.

Then, one day, she came sad-faced to the river. No singing or joking would make her smile.

I asked, "What troubles you so, my child?"

"There is a ball tonight, but I am not to go," she said, looking so miserable, my heart nearly snapped in two. "Vitaline and Mamma will go. But Mamma says I am lazy."

"Does it mean so much to you, this ball?"

"Oh, yes, *Nannin'!*" she cried. "It is a birthday *fèt'* for Paul, Monsieur Thibault's son. He is so handsome and well spoken, he is like a prince. Yet he is kind."

"Do not cry, dear one," I said, hugging her. "Tonight you will go to the ball."

"For true?"

"Upon my soul, I promise this," I said. Though I was fearful of risking so much when I had no plan.

But her smile lightened my heart. As she gathered up her laundry, I heard her singing.

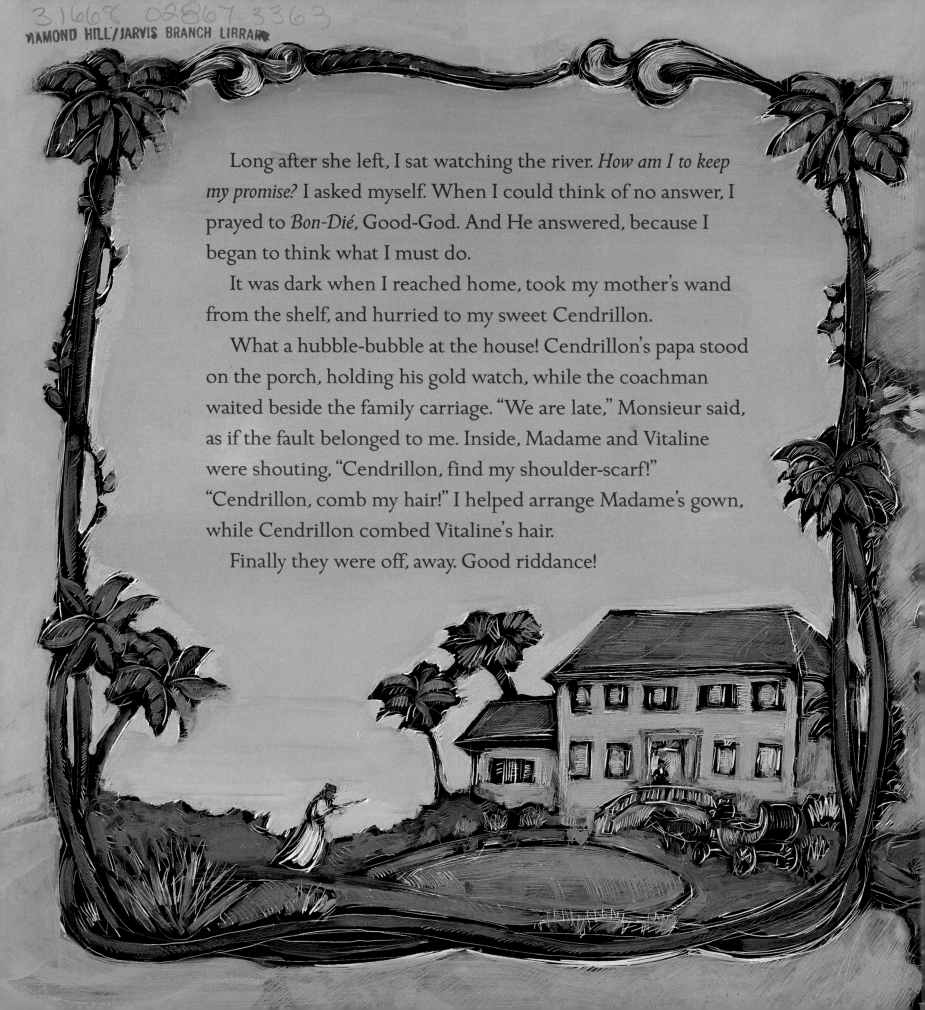

31668 02867 3363

MAMOND HILL/JARVIS BRANCH LIBRARY

Long after she left, I sat watching the river. *How am I to keep my promise?* I asked myself. When I could think of no answer, I prayed to *Bon-Dié*, Good-God. And He answered, because I began to think what I must do.

It was dark when I reached home, took my mother's wand from the shelf, and hurried to my sweet Cendrillon.

What a hubble-bubble at the house! Cendrillon's papa stood on the porch, holding his gold watch, while the coachman waited beside the family carriage. "We are late," Monsieur said, as if the fault belonged to me. Inside, Madame and Vitaline were shouting, "Cendrillon, find my shoulder-scarf!" "Cendrillon, comb my hair!" I helped arrange Madame's gown, while Cendrillon combed Vitaline's hair.

Finally they were off, away. Good riddance!

Upon the instant, I told Cendrillon, "Now *you* will go to the ball."

"But I have no carriage," she protested. "I have no gown."

"Go into the garden and pick a *fruit à pain*," I said.

The child looked at me as if she thought, *My poor nannin' has gone mad*. But she found a big, round breadfruit.

I tapped this three times—*to, to, to!*—with my wand, and it became a gilded coach.

So far so good!

Cendrillon gasped, but I told her, "Do not waste your breath on questions; we still have much to do."

To, to, to! Six *agoutis* in a cage became six splendid carriage horses. *To, to, to!* Five brown field lizards became five tall footmen. *To, to, to!* A plump *manicou* was changed to a coachman.

Then I tapped Cendrillon. Her poor calico dress was changed to a trailing gown of sky-blue velvet. Upon her head sat a turban just as blue, pinned with a *tremblant,* pin of gold. She had a silk shoulder-scarf of pale rose, rings in her ears, bracelets, and a necklace of four strands of gold beads, bigger than peas.

Upon her feet were elegant pink slippers, embroidered with roses. It was enough to hurt my eyes to look at my darling.

Finally, I turned my washerwoman's shift into a fine red dress. I would chaperone Cendrillon, as suited a proper young lady.

Away we went, over the bridge, through the town,
along the shore to the *granmaison* of Monsieur Thibault.
Just before we stepped down from our carriage, I
warned Cendrillon, "The magic lasts only a short time.
We must leave before the midnight bell is rung."

"Yes, *Nannin'*," she promised.

What a grand entrance Cendrillon made! All eyes turned toward her and could not turn away. I heard whispers all around: "Who is that pretty girl?" "Look how fine her clothes are!" "Did she come from France?"

Even Cendrillon's stepmother and sister did not recognize the two of us, though they peered crossly at us.

Then Paul, his eyes blazing with love-fire, asked her to dance. And he refused to dance with any other. I know. I watched as I ate. Oh, what fine food I helped myself to, as I watched the handsome couple. Even chocolate sherbet.

Cendrillon was so happy, and I was happy seeing her so, that we forgot to mark the time. Suddenly, I heard distant bells strike the first chime of midnight.

Astonishing all with my rudeness, I grabbed Cendrillon's hand and cried, "It is nearly midnight! We must go!"

For a moment, I feared she would not obey. Then she turned, and we ran toward the door.

Paul cried, "Wait! I do not even know your name!"

He ran after us, but guests and servants, confused by such running and shouting, blocked his way. As it was, we barely escaped to our carriage because Cendrillon stumbled on the stair. She had to leave behind one embroidered slipper.

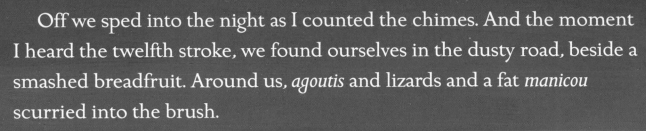

Off we sped into the night as I counted the chimes. And the moment
I heard the twelfth stroke, we found ourselves in the dusty road, beside a
smashed breadfruit. Around us, *agoutis* and lizards and a fat *manicou*
scurried into the brush.

We walked home like two ragged washerwomen. Our fine clothes
were gone—all except Cendrillon's one pink slipper.

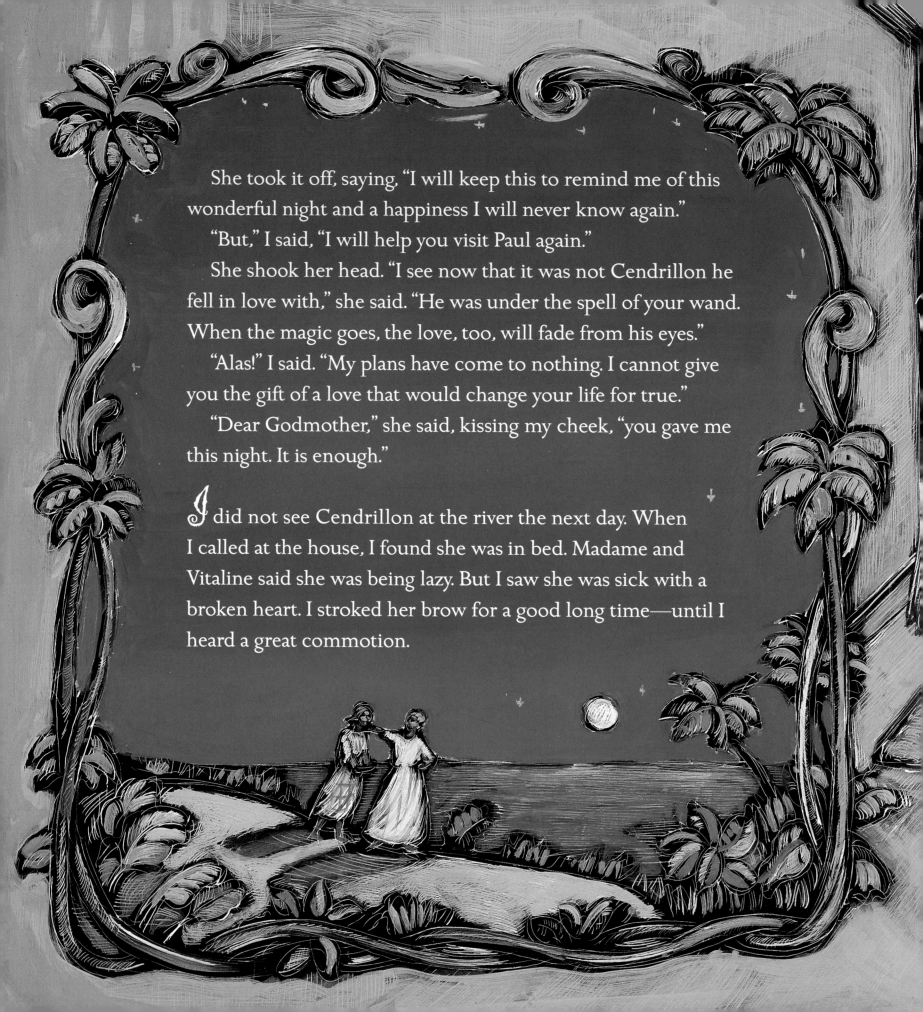

She took it off, saying, "I will keep this to remind me of this wonderful night and a happiness I will never know again."

"But," I said, "I will help you visit Paul again."

She shook her head. "I see now that it was not Cendrillon he fell in love with," she said. "He was under the spell of your wand. When the magic goes, the love, too, will fade from his eyes."

"Alas!" I said. "My plans have come to nothing. I cannot give you the gift of a love that would change your life for true."

"Dear Godmother," she said, kissing my cheek, "you gave me this night. It is enough."

I did not see Cendrillon at the river the next day. When I called at the house, I found she was in bed. Madame and Vitaline said she was being lazy. But I saw she was sick with a broken heart. I stroked her brow for a good long time—until I heard a great commotion.

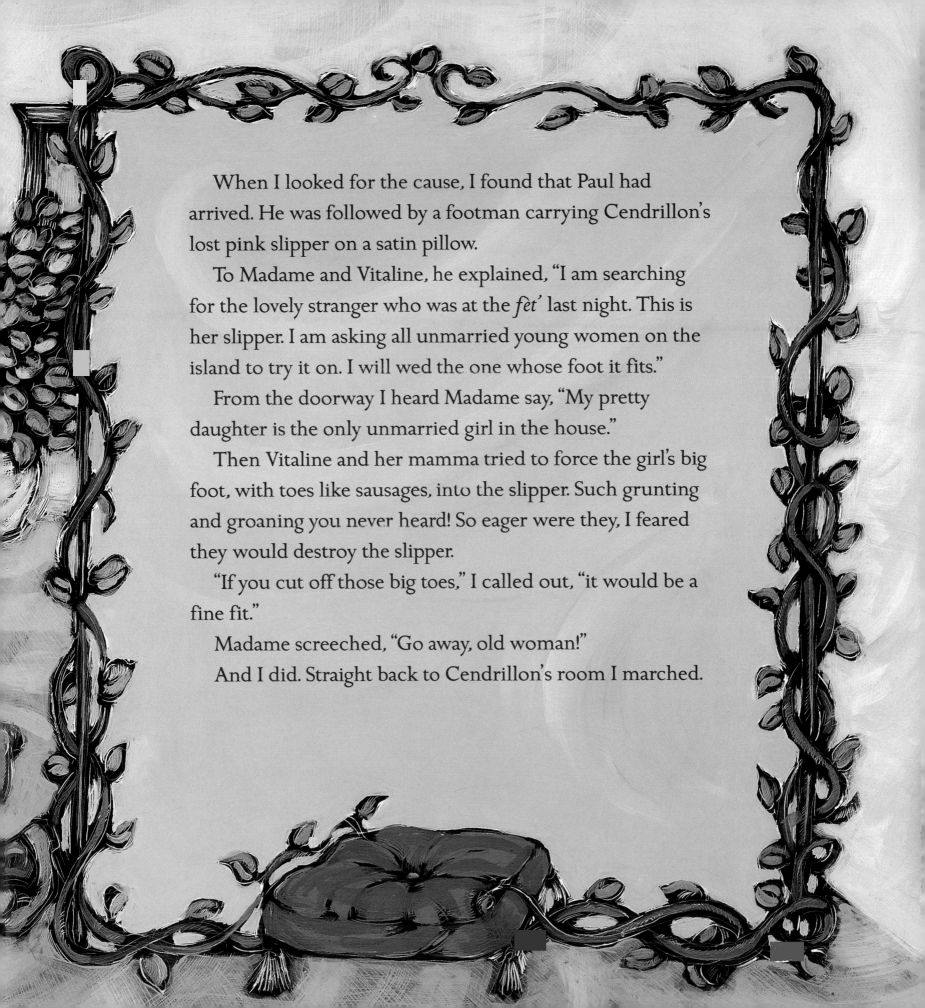

When I looked for the cause, I found that Paul had arrived. He was followed by a footman carrying Cendrillon's lost pink slipper on a satin pillow.

To Madame and Vitaline, he explained, "I am searching for the lovely stranger who was at the *fèt'* last night. This is her slipper. I am asking all unmarried young women on the island to try it on. I will wed the one whose foot it fits."

From the doorway I heard Madame say, "My pretty daughter is the only unmarried girl in the house."

Then Vitaline and her mamma tried to force the girl's big foot, with toes like sausages, into the slipper. Such grunting and groaning you never heard! So eager were they, I feared they would destroy the slipper.

"If you cut off those big toes," I called out, "it would be a fine fit."

Madame screeched, "Go away, old woman!"

And I did. Straight back to Cendrillon's room I marched.

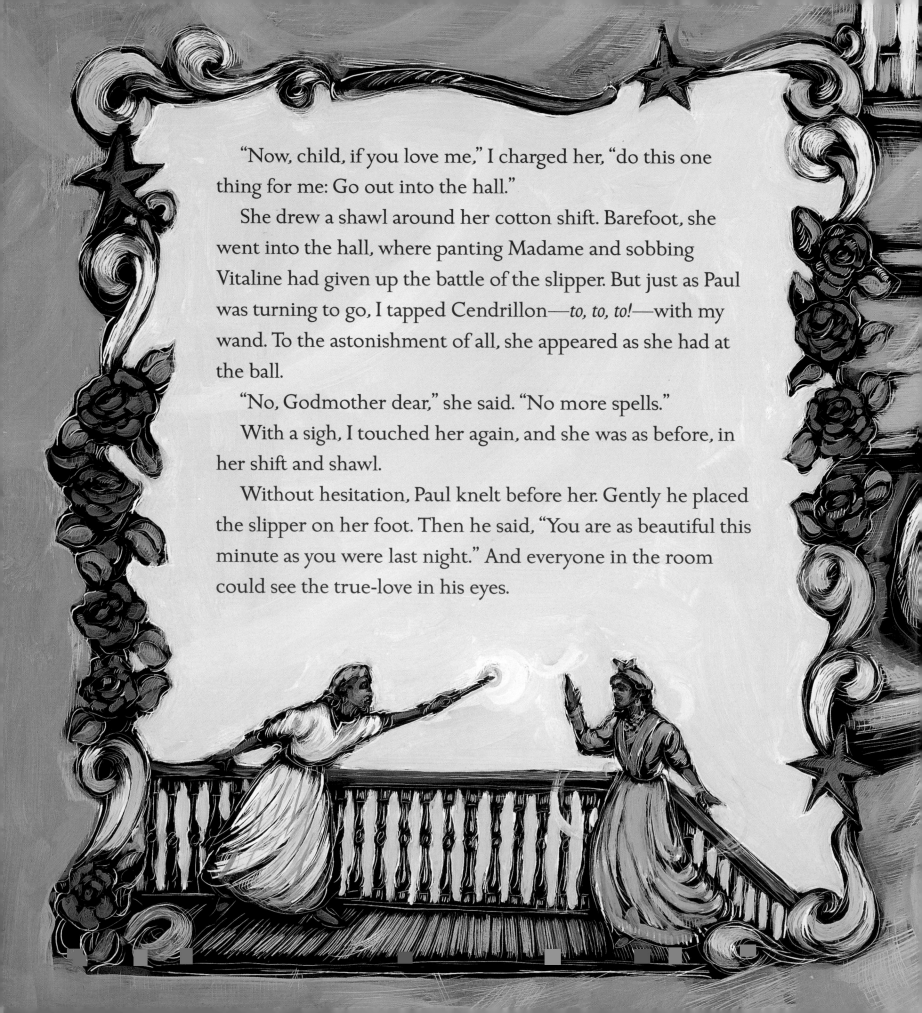

"Now, child, if you love me," I charged her, "do this one thing for me: Go out into the hall."

She drew a shawl around her cotton shift. Barefoot, she went into the hall, where panting Madame and sobbing Vitaline had given up the battle of the slipper. But just as Paul was turning to go, I tapped Cendrillon—*to, to, to!*—with my wand. To the astonishment of all, she appeared as she had at the ball.

"No, Godmother dear," she said. "No more spells."

With a sigh, I touched her again, and she was as before, in her shift and shawl.

Without hesitation, Paul knelt before her. Gently he placed the slipper on her foot. Then he said, "You are as beautiful this minute as you were last night." And everyone in the room could see the true-love in his eyes.

Cendrillon and Paul were married soon after this. Even the king and queen of France never had such a wedding! The guests ate and danced and sang and ate again for three days.

I know because I was there. I danced the *gwo-kā* and ate nine helpings of chocolate sherbet and came away only to tell you this tale.

Glossary of French Creole Words and Phrases

agouti (ah-GOO-tee): a rodent, something like a guinea pig, with long legs and hoof-like claws ideal for running

bébé (BEEYH-beeyh): baby

blanchisseuse (blahn-SHEEZ-seuz): a washerwoman

bonjou' (BOH-zhew): good day, hello

Bon-Dié (bohn-DEHW) [pronounced as one word]: the Good Lord

Cendrillon (SOHN-dree-yhon): the French form of Cinderella

fèt' (FET): a party, celebration

fruit à pain (FREE-ya pan) [pronounced as two words]: breadfruit

granmaison (grahn-MAY-zohn): a manor house

gwo-kā (Gwoh-KAH): literally, "big drum"; a lively dance, the music, and the instrument played

manicou (MAN-ee-coo): an opposum

Mer des Antilles (MEHR de-ZON-teeyl) [pronounced as two words]: literally, "Sea of the Antilles," the islands of the West Indies: the Caribbean Sea

monsieur (MONH-sur): mister, sir; the French form of polite address

nannin' (non-NIHN): godmother

pauv' ti Cendrillon (pov tee SOHN-dree-yohn): poor little Cinderella

Paul (POWL): a man's name

Prospèrine (Pros SPER-in): a woman's name

Thibault (TEE-bowl): a family name

tremblant (TRHEM-blahn): a gold pin

Vitaline (VEE-tah-leen): a woman's name

Note: I have retained the proper French, rather than Creolized, spellings of "Cendrillon" and "Monsieur," since they are more familiar usages, and would reflect the parents' pretensions and concern with their French ancestry. In island Creole, "Cinderella" would be written out "Sandriyon," though pronounced the same as "Cendrillon"; "Monsieur" would be "Missié" (MIH-seeyh).

Author's Note

This story is loosely based on the French Creole tale "Cendrillon," in Turiault's nineteenth-century *Creole Grammar*. That version follows the basic outline of Perrault's "Cinderella," while incorporating elements of West Indian culture and costume.

I have expanded the tale considerably, drawing on details of life on the island of Martinique, culled from such sources as Lafcadio Hearn's *Two Years in the French West Indies* (New York and London: Harper & Brothers Publishers, 1890) and Patrick Chamoiseau's *Creole Folktales* (New York: The New Press, 1994), translated from the French by Linda Coverdale.

The decision to tell the story from the godmother's point of view arose over the course of rewriting. She seemed a natural storyteller for a narrative that grows out of Creole oral tradition, and her unique perspective allowed me to add a fresh wrinkle to this timeless tale.

Special thanks to Myriam M. Dahomé for her help with the Creole vocabulary and pronunciation guide

First Aladdin Paperbacks edition January 2002

Text copyright © 1998 by Robert D. San Souci
Illustrations copyright © 1998 by Brian Pinkney

Aladdin Paperbacks
An imprint of Simon & Schuster
Children's Publishing Division
1230 Avenue of the Americas
New York, NY 10020

All rights reserved, including the right of
reproduction in whole or in part in any form.

Also available in a Simon & Schuster Books for Young Readers hardcover edition.
Designed by Paul Zakris
The text of this book was set in 16-point Golden Cockerel
The illustrations were rendered in scratchboard, luma dyes, gouache, and oil paints.
Printed in Hong Kong
10 9 8 7 6 5 4 3 2 1

The Library of Congress has cataloged the hardcover edition as follows:
San Souci, Robert D.
Cendrillon : a Caribbean Cinderella / Robert D. San Souci ; illustrated by Brian Pinkney.
p.   cm.
Summary: A Creole variant of the familiar Cinderella tale set in the Caribbean and narrated by the godmother who helps Cendrillon find true love.
ISBN 0-689-80668-X (hc.)
[1. Fairy Tales. 2. Folklore—France.] I. Pinkney, J. Brian, ill. II. Perrault, Charles, 1628–1703. Cendrillon, English.
PZ8.S248Ce 1998
398.2—dc21
96-53142
ISBN 0-689-84888-9 (Aladdin pbk.)